First Printing, 2001 Printed in Hong Kong

Text and illustrations copyright © 2001 by Karen Salmansohn. All rights reserved. No part of this book may be reproduced in any form without the written permission of the publisher, except in the case of brief quotations embodied in critical articles or reviews. Tricycle Press, P.O. Box 7123, Berkeley, California 94707.

www.tenspeed.com
Book design by Karen Salmansohn.
Library of Congress Cataloging-in-Publication Data
Salman sohn, Karen.

One puppy, three tales /by Karen Salmansohn -- rambles on. Old twelve-year-... summaria... Alexandra... 2 Old twelve-year-... Alexandra tries to understand her relationship with her father and her best friend (and starts)...

...(hard cover) -- ... Interpersonal relations. 2. Friendship -- ... Motherhood. 8.

...and daughters. 4. friendship-- I. I. Title. [E]--dc21 ... 345 on 2001 ... 2001010-0290

ISBN 1-58246-034-5

2 3 4 5 6 7 - 05 04 03 02 01

NOTE: Hmm. It seems not only does Alexandra ramble on, so does the publisher cachem...

ALEXANDRA! Rambles On!

ONE PUPPY, THREE TALES

by Karan Salmansohn

Tricycle Press
Berkeley | Toronto

There are **many things** I'm still waiting for **my dad** to tell me.

For example:

Why can **dogs** understand our language, but we can't understand theirs?

Does a **parrot** really know what it is saying when it talks? And does **my brother, Howie,** really know what he is saying when he talks? And if so, why does he say so many stupid things?

My mom loves it when I ask her questions like these. She answers me

BOW WOW.

TRANSLATION: Is the speed of the ball affected more by its weight or size?

Polly wants a cracker.

TRANSLATION: Polly REALLY wants a pizza, but will settle for a stale cracker.

in a **MOM-o-Logue.** But every time I ask my dad a question, he gives me the **same answer:** "I'm very busy right now, Alexandra, I'll talk to you later."

Which brings me to some **NEW** questions.

Some NEW Questions:
- When is **later** anyway?
- Is it sooner than a **fortnight?**
- Less than a **fortmorning?**
- And what are those, anyway?
- Will later ever come?
- Will it come by the time I reach **age 13** ...or **page 49?**
- Why is dad spelled backward still dad— and mom still mom—but brother is **rehtorb?**

TALE #1

What is weird? Weird is what?

It is now 7:03 P.M. Do you know where your mother is? • I don't. • My mom was supposed to be home at 6 P.M. — one hour ago — or four bracelets in "bracelet-making time." (Note: That's how many bracelets I've beaded since waiting for her.) • Right now I am in my room, putting the last little pink bead on this fourth bracelet (an orange and pink one) and wonderin where my mom could be. She promised me she'd be home from rehearsal early tonight — with my Halloween costume — because I have this cool Halloween party that I am **SUPPOSED TO BE AT — IN UNDER**

CHOCOLATE

achem!

LATE as in what my mom is!

HAPPY PUMPKIN!

BLUE PUMPKIN!

Grrr rrr rrr rrr rrr

ONE HOUR! • Yikes! • **Where** is my
mom with my costume already?! •
Okay. I am giving my mom two
more bracelets to get here before I
get really mad — like Grrrrr mad.
I decide to make this next bracelet
orange and black in honor of
Halloween. I love Halloween — and
not just for the **FREE CHOCOLATE**
(yum!). But also the way I see it,
any day where I get to be someone
other than myself is fine by me. •
This year I found my favorite
Halloween costume ever: **a**

**glamourous movie
star costume!**

PARTY

1
hour

another
the

ME →
without
costume

pink bead

bracelet ↓

And my favorite part of getting to be a movie star is (no, not the rhine-stone studded sunglasses!) – the **HAIR!** I am going to get to wear this cool wig of **long straight blond hair.** Real movie star hair. • My real hair is more of the peasant sort: dark, curly, and very moody. • Every morning when I wake up, I look in the mirror nervously, scared of what personality my hair will take on for that day. If my hair has decided to be super curly (meaning super weirdo) I find **myself totally** dreading school. • My

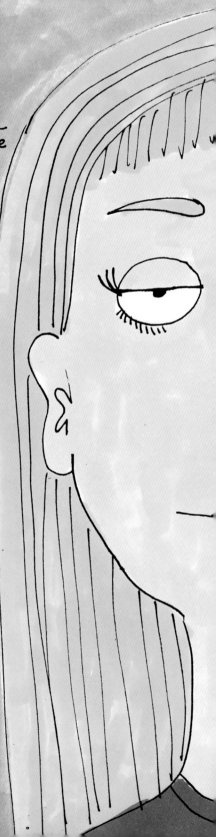

mother's hair is like mine. She tells me, "You know, there are people out there who pay lots of money to have hair like ours. Some day — just like me — you'll be glad to have curly hair." • **Puh-lease.** • Vicki Stone, the girl who invited me to tonight's cool Halloween party, has the hair I dream of having — blond, straight hair so **shiny** you'd think you could see yourself in it, if you stood in front of it and stared really hard. Vicki, in my opinion, is the coolest girl in school. She looks **like an ad for Perfect Girl Shampoo.**

• And not only is Vicki really cool, so is Vicki's mom. • I met Vicki's mom at this year's school fund-raiser. She—like Vicki—has that beautiful hair. Plus she dressed very classy, in this pretty navy suit, and she baked theee best **Lemon Meltaways** ever— perfect amounts of lemoniness and meltability. EVERYTHING about Vicki's mom is as perfect as her meltaways— and as opposite from MY mom as you can get.

• My mom showed up that day LATE as usu... and looking so..., so... so... NON-mom-ish. • First of all, there's her totally NON-mom hair. • Next of all, she wore this NON-mom outfit - a black leotard top and this weird **zebra print** skirt. I ask you: What kind of mom wears **zebra**

And OF COURSE mom did not bake anything for the fundraiser. Instead, she set up a table where she offered to teach people...

... YOGA! My mom (GET THIS...) then took off her zebra skirt and stood there wearing only a black leotard yoga outfit. (How embarrassing, right?)

Then she twisted herself into...

... weird yoga positions and tried to get people to sign up with her so she could show **them** how to twist into weird positions, too. • She kept shouting things like, "Okay, bring on the next victim!" really, really **LOUDLY.** It was soooo embarrassing! I swear, I turned the color of these beads right here! (uh-oh! I'm now starting bracelet #2! **WHERE IS SHE?**)

Mom's big problem: She does not know how to act her age.

"I still feel like a teenager," my mom insists. "I don't feel like a mom."

My mom has even told me she doesn't want me to think of her as "**my mom**" but as "**my friend**." But I don't want a mom who is my friend. A mom is supposed to be **A MOM**. It's sort of like how you would not want to use a lamp as a **chair** or a **pencil** as an **umbrella**. My mom insists she cannot stop herself from acting non-mom-ish — all **loud** and **goofy** and **embarrassing**.

"I'm a **cabaret lounge singer**," she explains

Not a chair, either

uh? As if **that's** an explanation!
Note: What that means is that my mom sings
ngs, not while standing, like a **normal person**,
ut while **sitting on top of a piano**. She calls
erself a "**CROONER**" which I guess means "a
erson who sings songs while sitting on top
f a piano."
"The breeze is chasing the zephyr, "**mom croons.**
The moon is chasing the sea, the bull is chasing
he heifer, but nobody's chasing me."
Note to mom: maybe nobody's chasing you because
ou're wearing a **dorky zebra print outfit.**
I don't mean to be mean. But I'm mad at
ny mom for being **sooo late** with my costume—and
or being **so embarrassing!** I hate having **Zebra**
Mom come to meet me at school.

zebra
from
Ze front

I've read a lot ab
zebras, and let me te
you: **zebras are ver**
weird animals. Not on!
do no two zebRas
look alike, No two ac
alike.

Some people think zebr
are just like horses with
stripes. But they are **very**
different. Zebras are
more wild and less oper
to suggestion from other.
A zebra will only do what
the zebra itself wants to
do. That's why a horse can
be trained, but a zebra

cannot. And that's why you hear about **Horse Whisperers** but not Zebra Whisperers.

(**Question:** If a Horse Whisperer is a person who speaks with horses, would a **Horse Crooner** be a person who speaks to horses while sitting on a piano?)

Anyway, I often wish I had **a normal Horse Mom** - like Vicki's mom - a mom who is sleek and graceful and gets along well with others. Instead I got stuck with **Zebra Mom**, who bugs me and embarrasses me.

Zebra from ze rear

SOME STUFF THAT BUGS ME AND EM-BARRASSES ME ABOUT MY MOM:

① (Or rather, make that number ⑥, because I think I already listed about 5 things, so it's...)

⑥ My mom is always doing spacey stuff, like slipping up and calling me "Howie." (**Note:** I get back at her by calling her "Dad.")

⑦ My mom is always confusing me with her. She hates tomatoes, so I must hate tomatoes. She loves zebra print, so I must love zebra print. Once she even got me weird zebra print shoes, then expected me to wear them!

"Mom, puh-lease," I told her. "They are like so weird." • "I know," said my mom, "Aren't they just great?" Basically, my mom just does not get it.

WEIRD DOES NOT = GREAT. Weird = being not normal. And what I want = being normal. What I want = a mom who = a mom!

My best friend, Liz, tells me I should appreciate my mom just as she is. Liz thinks my mom is VERY cool. But I think that's because:

① My mom once told Liz she looks like Winona Ryder—and **Liz loves Winona.** Liz even named her cat Winona.

② Liz doesn't have a mom at all. Liz's mom passed away when she was seven. So my mom has sort of become Liz's replacement mom.

• Liz is my **VBF** - my **Very Best Friend**. And Liz is not only close to me, she's also **CLOSE TO ME**. She lives right next door. I love that. I have Liz so close by to talk to - and that I can talk to Liz about **ANYTHING** and not feel like she is looking at me like I have smudged ink all over my face. • Liz and I talk about **EVERYTHING.** stuff like:

① Liz's **crush** on this boy, **Karl.**
② my **crush** on this boy, **Max.**
③ who we think is **cool** and **pretty** and **why.**

• I think Vicki is the prettiest and coolest girl in our school - and her mom is the most coolest mom ever. • "You and your mom are waaay cooler," Liz has told me. "I think Vicki and her mom are BOTH totally **BORING!**" • But I think Liz just told me that because:

① mom said that Winona Ryder look-a-like thing.
② Vicki **did not invite** Liz to her Halloween party.

• Liz claims she did not want to go to Vicki's **"STUPID"** (Note: That's Liz'z word) party. • "It's probably going to be very boring," Liz has said, "just like Vicki and her boring mom." • But I don't know... I **doubt** Liz thinks that **FOR REAL.**

I just think Liz is **jealous** that I am goi
to Vicki's party - that is if I   am
ever going. I'm almost done with th
second bracelet, and my mom—wha
that? Could it be? • Yes! **FINALLY**,
mom is coming through the fron-
door. It took 5½ bracelets, but
FINALLY, she's home. • "Who wants
ice cream?" my mom
yells. • "Yeah!" my dad and
Howie both yell back
from the living room where
they are watch- ing a basketball game. • We all run into
the kitchen to greet

MY NEW COSTUME / NOTHING

my mom, who is standing there **WITH**
ice cream but **WITHOUT** costume! • "where
is my costume?" • "what?" says my mom.
"I'm so sorry, honey. Rehearsal ran late,
then I totally forgot. • What I am
thinking is: **Grrrrrr.** • What comes out
of my mouth is: "mom! How could you?
Now the store is closed and I have

NOTHING to wear to Vicki's party. Now I can't go!!". "I'm so sorry, honey," says my mom. "You want to go see a movie instead?". "I do," says my brother. • "That's a great idea," says my dad. • What I am now thinking is: Grrrrrrrrrrrrrrrrrrrr-rrrrrrrrrrrrrrrrrrrrrr-rrrrr-

MY NEW MOOD

DARK

rrrrr!." "I don't want to SEE movie stars, I want to dress up like one!" I say, then run to my room and slam the door really, really loudly. I am so angry! Should I go to Vicki's party without a costume or should I not go to Vicki's party at all? I think about calling Liz. But I know what she'll say: "Why would you even want to go to Vicki's stupid party anyway?" But I DO want to go. I REALLY want to go. And so I'm REALLY angry at mom. • I hear a KNOCK.

"Honey," says my mom. • "Don't come in," I say. • The door opens ANYWAY. • Grrrrr. "Look what I found," says my mom, sticking her **brightly colored Japanese bathrobe** in my face. • "Why are you showing me your robe?" I ask. • "It's your new **geisha girl costume**," says my mom. "For Vicki's party. And we could **paint your face white, and stick chopsticks in your hair.**" • "I...er..." • "Try it on," says my mom. • I take off my sweats...and slip on her Japanese robe. Before I can say anything, my mom starts powdering my face with lots of makeup. I stare at myself in the mirror. In the end I think I look **kind of sort of kind of maybe** pretty cool. • "So?" says mom, smiling this big goofy smile—the kind of smile you get when you stick a quarter of an orange in your mouth. • "So, what do you think?" she asks. • "I think maybe I'll go to Vicki's party after all." • My mom tries to put her arms around me, but I push her off. • "However," I say, "I **ALSO** think that I am **STILL** mad at you—and will be—for at least **six more bracelets.**" • "What?" says my mom. • "Never mind," I say. "Let's go." • My mom and I head to the car, where my brother and dad are already waiting. They drop me off at Vicki's house on their way to the movies. • "See you afterwards,

darling!" my mom yells and waves as they drive off.
• Vicki has a pretty house (duh! of course!) with lots
of white, and a pretty powder blue door. I ring Vicki's
doorbell. (It even makes a pretty ding dong sound.) •
Vicki's mom answers. • "Yes, can I help you?" she asks.
• "I'm here for the Halloween party," I explain. • "The
Halloween party?" • "Am I early?" • "Late, dear. I'm
afraid the party was yesterday." • "yesterday?." I
repeat. • **How did this happen?** Did my mom write the
party down on the calendar in the **wrong space?** Did
I space and tell my mom the **wrong date?** Am I
becoming as ditzy as my mom? **WHO** should I be mad
at? me? Or my mom? • I decide either way I should
be mad at my mom, because my mom is slowly and
sneakily turning me into her. Yes, I am becoming my
mom. Yes, **THIS,** it seems is now my **new Halloween costume.**
• "Oh, well," I say and try to smile. • My **NEW goal for**
the moment: look cool, calm, and collected. My **NEW**
goal for life: I will not turn into my spacey, weird
mom. **I will not turn into my spacey weird mom.**
• Though it's hard to look cool, calm, and collected
(or nonspacey and nonweird) while one is dressed like a
geisha girl on someone's doorstep. • (Somebody kill
me now, please!) • "Well, sweetie," Vicki's mom
says, "Vicki is out with her dad. Why don't you
call your mom and have her pick you up?" • " my
mom's not home," I say. "Nobody is. They all
went to a movie. They won't be home for, like,

two hours."•"Oh, too bad Vicki isn't here. But
come in."• I look at Vicki's mom's sweet
face and think how much I wish Vicki's
normal mom were **MY** mom. I wish I had a
NORMAL mom **FOREVER**.• She brings me into the
kitchen where there are two other women —
two other normal mom types — seated at a
big round table. I have hit the **normal mom**
jackpot! Both these new
normal moms are wearing
pretty blue **NORMAL**
dresses — like real mom
— with not a zebra stripe
in sight.•"Her mother con-
fused the day of the party
Vicki's mom explains.•"Oh
dear," says one of the normal moms.
•I happily take a seat next to Vicki's mom.
On the table is a plate of her **lemon melt-**
aways. Together all four of us sit, eat
meltaways, watch TV, and talk recipes. Or
at least three out of four of us talk recipes,
while one of us (me!) just listens to: oven
preheating recommendations, favorite
ingredients, and the difference between
Pyrex and Stonewall baking dishes. **That's**
when I discover what normal moms really

A MOUTH EATING A LEMON MELTAWAY

think/say. And what I discover is: Normal moms are **really boring.** • "I always add a teaspoon of baking soda to my cornbread," says one normal mom. • "Really!" the others gasp. • "I like to mix in brown sugar with white sugar in my sugar cookies," says another normal mom. • "My, how clever!"one says. •"What a great idea!" says another. **As if!**• I look at the lock, and suddenly I **annot wait** for my two hours to pass. These two ours now seem like a life- ime. That's when I wonder:

A BORED MOUTH YAWNING

What would a lifetime with a normal mom feel like? Just the thought of this makes me thirsty. • "Excuse me, Mrs. Stone," I say to Vicki's mom. "Can I please have some more uice?" • "I'm Mrs. White," the woman nswers. "That's Mrs. Stone, over there." I look at them both, then at the

...third woman, and I can't tell any of the three normal moms apart. They all look so much alike. Like

...one big blue blur.

I watch them, watch me, and as they now I see how they all even raise their drinking glasses at the same time! • Suddenly, instead of seeing these women as Horse Moms - acting like a sleek pack of horses - I see them all as ants - like ants on a hillside, ants that all look the same, and all do the same ant things, all together.

I've read a lot about
ant behavior.
It is called
"Alleo Mimetic Behavior" and it means

"When animals in a group
all start to think and
behave in the same way."

Alleomimetic Behavior
means: **There are no
unique thinkers or
doers in the
group.**

No one ant
is capable of thinking
or doing something unique
that it likes,
like yoga or sitting on top
of pianos crooning.

An ant
just does what everybody else
is doing just because
everybody else is
doing it.
**How boring
is that?**

Then I think:
   MAYBE Liz is right.
MAYBE
   I should **be glad to have
a zebra Mom...**

and not some...

      ...Alleomimetic Ant Mom.

when those two hours finally pass
      and my mom actually shows up, I
am actually glad to see her
      FOR A CHANGE.

      ...I am
      EVEN actually
         sort of maybe
   even kinda glad to see
         her **zebra
            coat.**

Later that
      night
   when
      I get home,
I pull out all the
black and white
beads I have,

and I make
my mom the
prettiest,
coolest, niftiest

black and white bracelet EVER.

Another Question:

Why were big, huge **DINOSAURS** not able to survive the test of time, but teeny, tiny termites were? Yes, **termites** have been around since the time of dinosaurs. Meaning? A termite is harder to kill than a dinosaur. It seems a teeny termite is **very strong!** It can chew through houses and trees— and maybe even dinosaurs! And if you try to poison a termite, it has this **super strong tummy** that can resist most poisons! (**QUESTION:** Shouldn't termite be spelled **"TERMIGHT"**?) Probably if you tried to poison a huge dinosaur, it would fall over and **become history** which I guess explains why dinosaurs **are** history, and termites are **not**. But there is one way for sure to kill a termite. Here it is. **HOW TO KILL A TERMITE:** Take the termite away from its other termite friends. Then the termite will die. **IT'S LIKE THIS:** A termite gets a lot of its strength and energy from being around other termites. It needs to be around **its friends** or else it won't have the energy to flutter its wings. It will just sit there until it **dies**. Even just having **one friend** next to it gives it some strength to **fly!** I relate. That's the way I feel about **iz.** Whenever Liz is around, I always feel **more fluttery.** Once when I was home sick, Liz came by to visit, and because she was sitting next to me on the bed, I suddenly felt a lot more energetic, which is something that would happen to a sick termite if a termite came near it. Sometimes, all I have to do is see Liz and I feel all fluttery.

NOTE #1: These dots are termites eating a yummy dino-snack.

Note #2: No dinosaurs were hurt or killed in the making of this drawing!

TALE #2

FREE TO BE ME
...or does being me have a price? and if so, how much should I charge?

Note: See the happy face? I drew Liz upside down so she would look like she's smiling even though she's un-happy.

Liz and I have now started our own jewelry business. • Liz and I love making **beaded bracelets, necklaces, earrings, and rings,** which everyone is **always** complimenting us on sooo much— and asking us if they can buy them from us— well, Liz and I decided we should sell **OUR** jewelry during lunchtime. • So we are. • And ... we've already sold **19 pieces! OUR BIG PLAN:** Make enough money to buy ourselves computers! • **OUR BIGGER PLAN:** Set up a web site and sell our jewelry on the **Internet!** • How amazing would that be? huh? • And just last week Vicki told me how much she loved my bracelets—

and how much she wanted one – a pink and orange one, like the one I was wearing. She tried it on and it fit her perfectly so I told her she could have it. She asked if she could have it for **free** since it was kinda used, and she's my friend, so I said okay. However, this seems to be **NOT OKAY** according to Liz. Liz is in my room now making bracelets with me, and Liz is very (VERY) mad. She is telling me how she is feeling while waving her hands a lot as she talks. "You **can't** just **give away** our bracelets!" Liz is saying. "Why?" I say. "You gave your sister, Rachel, a free one." "That's different," says Liz. "Rachel is my sister." "Well," I say. "**Vicki is a good friend.**" "Yeah, as if," says Liz. "Does Vicki ever call you just to say **absolutely nothing?**" "Huh?" I say. **So Liz says...**

●"For me, a **good friend** is some-one who calls you to say absolutely nothing-because they want absolutely nothing from you. Just to be your friend. And it seems like the **ONLY time** Vicki calls you is when she wants something, like help with her math homework. ●"Um," I say. ●"I don't t**r**ust Vicki," Liz continues. "She is not a nice person. She's **mean** to a lot of people at school, which also makes Vicki a big hypocrite, because she has this big sticker on her notebook that says: **MEAN PEOPLE SUCK.**"● Hmmm.● Maybe Liz has a teeny-tiny, bead-size point. Sometimes Vicki **is** mean to some people.● But Vicki doesn't mean **to be mean.** She's just picky about who she lets into her clique.

You see, there are these **cliques** in school. And you have to be just like the people in the clique to get in the **clique**. If you are different, then you must find a clique of people just like **YOU**. • Actually, it's a lot like how it is in the animal kingdom. I've read that animals have cliques, too. • Certain **FISH** will only swim with certain **FISH**. • Certain **birds** will only fly with certain **birds**. • certain **horses** will only gallop with certain **horses**. • And in our school, the **JOCKS** hang out with the **JOCKS**. • The **artsy kids** hang out with the **artsy kids**. The **cool kids** hang out with **cool kids**. • **MY PROBLEM?**

•I don't just have **one clique** I hang out with. I mainly hang out with Liz. We are our own **two-person clique**. Sometimes I wish I were in a **real** clique, only I don't even know which clique I'd want to be in.. • I ~~guess~~ I want to be in Vicki's **cool** clique. But I also want to be in the **artsy** clique and the **honors?** club clique.

•I have sooo many different kinds of people inside me. And I **never** know who I am going to be and when. With some people I am loud. With others I am quiet. With some I feel totally cool. With others I feel like a big geek. •Is it good to be so many different people? •Or is it bad? **And why is it?.** Sometimes I just change without even trying. •Maybe this, too, is an animal instinct thingie. • I've read how some animals can change to match up with whoever they are with.

Like if a chameleon were near a leopard, it would get spots. • Many fish have developed this thing where they first send out vibrations to see if you are in their "**special fish clique**," and if you are, you have to learn how to send back the same "**special top secret fish clique vibrations**." If you do, then they let you swim with them. • If you are left you don't, then out. • I relate. • I sometimes feel like I am trying to send out "**Special top secret clique vibrations**," with whatever clique I am with so I will not be left out. • So, I act more "**artsy**" when I am with my "**artsy**" friends - and more "**cool**" whenever I am hanging out with Vicki and her clique of **cool friends**. • I wish I didn't

...care what people think about me. Is that stupid?

   Ooops. I just cared what people think about me - again!

   Liz **never** cares what people think about her. Liz just cares about being Liz. **So Liz is always just Liz**, no matter who she is with. I wish I could be more like Liz. But then I would not be me, I'd be Liz... **Oh, I think my brain is going to explode!!!**

   Liz is more daring than me. For instance, Liz has three piercings in her right ear-lobe. And Liz wants to get a tattoo of a butterfly and maybe a bellybutton piercing - **but I would never have the guts.**

   "Why not?" Liz has asked me.

   "I'm afraid of what people would say - what my parents would say."

   "Well, if you want something deeply in your heart," Liz said, "**then you must follow your heart!**"

Liz is always telling me

I MUST FOLLOW MY HEART.

And I **want** to follow my heart. But sometimes I feel my heart is walking in a circle or a zigzag, and it's hard to follow my heart when it is going **so quickly all over the place**... here... no there... no over there... Yeesh. My heart seems to be **lost** a lot of the time. I guess this is why I don't know which clique I fit into... **and if I fit in anywhere!** I guess I don't really know myself at all! And if **I** don't know **me** — and I spend sooo much time with me — then... well... is it possible for **anybody** else to really know me, either? **HELP!**

Note: I think Liz is better at not caring what people think because she already faced one of the **scariest** things ever — watching her mom die. **Wow, huh?** I guess for Liz, after going through something as scary as that, **everything else** feels a lot less scary. (or at least that's what my mom guesses. My mom once told me that she thinks Liz is very gutsy because this **sad thing** made her **strong inside.** maybe. Liz **is** one of the **gutsiest** people I know. I'm thinking about this when...

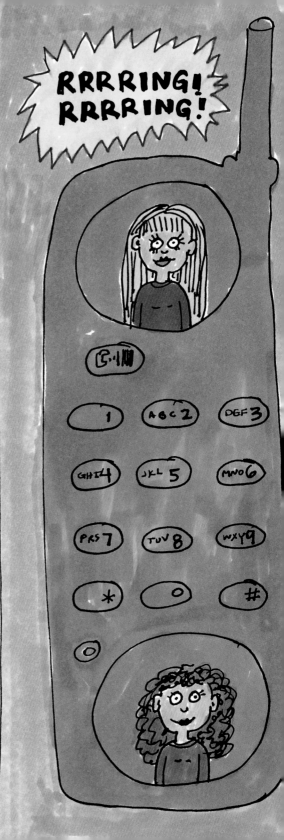

...the phone rings snapping me out of my thoughts.

I pick up.

"Hi, it's Vicki," says Vicki.

"Hi, Vicki," I say.

I give Liz this look— a look that says: **see,** Vicki **is** my pal. She's calling me just to talk. See?

See? See? See?

"How you doing?" asks Vicki.

"Good. And you?" I say.

"Good," says Vicki.

I keep staring at Liz and thinking:

SEE? SEE? SEE?

"So, I looove my new bracelet," says Vicki.

"Thanks," I say.

"I was wondering if you could give me a few more — for my boyfriend, Steve, and his whole football team, like about ten black and green ones, the same colors in their football jerseys," says Vicki.

"You want ten more bracelets?" I say.

I look at Liz again, only this time I am thinking: **uh-oh.**

Maybe Liz is right.

Maybe Vicki just **fakes** being **nice** when she wants something.

Hmmm. Could it be?

I take a deep breath. "Vicki," I say. "I was thinking. I know I gave you that one bracelet for free."

"And I **loooove** it. It's sooo pretty," says Vicki.

"Thanks," I say. "but I was thinking ... I am actually in business with Liz to sell these bracelets so we can make money to buy new computers. So, well, I'm going to have to charge you for any more bracelets. Especially since you want a lot of them."

"**Charge me?**" Vicki says.

"yeah. It's only fair. I mean, well, I think you should sorta kinda pay for them like everyone else at school."

"oh," says Vicki.

There's a long silence on the phone.

"Okay. Fine. Sure. Whatever," says Vicki.

"Thanks," I say. "You **do** understand, right?"

"Whatever," says Vicki.

But I have **no idea** what Vicki is thinking or feeling right now.

"Are you mad at me?" I ask.

☑ yes

cherry

no ☒

olive

yes no ☒

Vicki

"No sweetie," she says in a voice that is **sooo sweet**, it doesn't sound sweet at all. "So, anyway, gotta go."

"But... I..."

CLICK. Too late. She's hung up.

Ugh. Is Vicki just **faking being sweet** to me? Is Vicki going to run off and talk about me behind my back? Does Vicki still want to be my friend?

I **never** have any of these questions about Liz. I never feel like Liz is being fake nice. I **always** know just how Liz is feeling. Even if she's not feeling so good about me.

When Liz is angry, she tells me she's angry.

When Liz thinks I'm being an idiot because I give away free bracelets, she tells me I'm being an idiot.

"Hey, Liz," I say. →

"I just figured out what to look for **most** in a friend." →

"Someone who is truthful," I say. "People who say **truthful things** are the best-est, coolest friends to have." →

"**And** so are people who say something like that **right back**," I say. →

"**And** so are people who say something like that **right back** at someone who just said —" →

← "Yeah," says Liz.

← "Do tell," says Liz raising one eyebrow.

Liz looks at me and smiles. "And," says Liz, people who say something like that also are the **bestest, coolest friends.**" ←

"**And** so are people who say something like that **right back** at someone who said something **right back**." ←

"Oh, **SHUT UP!**" Liz says. "You're starting to get on my nerves."

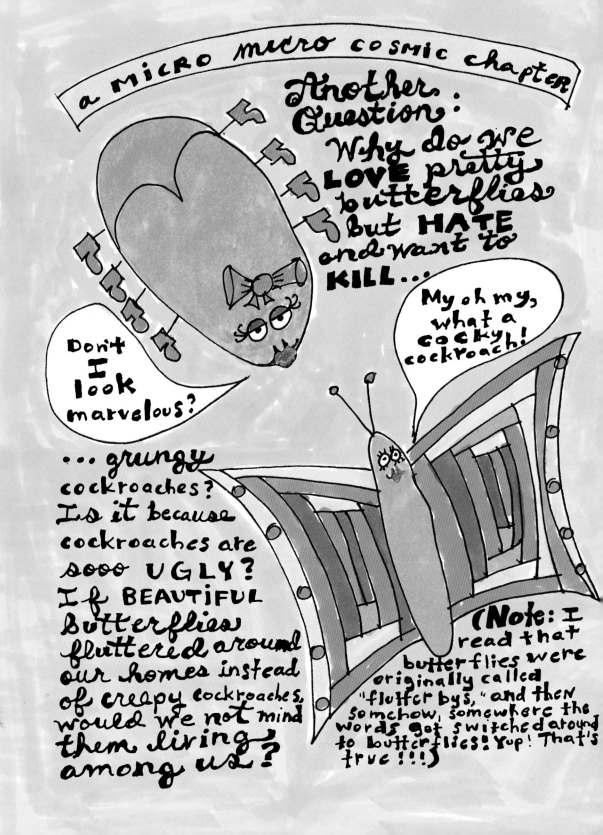

Okay.

So, remember back in the beginning, how my dad promised he'd answer my questions LATER? Well, I feel a lot of laters have already passed—WOOOSH right by—and my dad has yet to answer any questions! My dad has yet to tell me, why, in books a dog has four ways to talk: ① arf ② woof ③ bow-wow ④ ruff. But a pig only says: ① oink. And a cow only says: ① moooo. And my dad has yet to tell me why people say they have a frog in their throat...

And my dad has yet to tell me... I love you, Alexandra. ...oops... I know that was **not a** question. That was a statement. But it's a statement I sometimes sorta kinda question. (uh-oh. Just thinking about it now gives me a ← **PORCUPINE** in my throat!)

...and butterflies in their tummy. why not a **PORCUPINE IN THEIR THROAT,** and armadillos in their tummy?

I know, I know, I know,
I **know**. (I even **KNOW** !)
My mom has explained
this all to me a ga-
zillion times: My dad
(says my mom) is just
not the type to say
"mushy-gushy-love-
things." My dad
(says my mom) is just
not a mushy-gushy
kinda guy. He's a senior
V.P. in charge of marketing.
Whatever that means.
Actually, what it means is:
He works really, really hard.
So I barely get to talk to him.
And when my dad does have
time to talk, what
he most wants to
talk about is...

BASKET-
BALL.

"Oakley's gonna
chew up Barkley
when Phoenix...

comes to town," says my dad to my brother, Howie. • "It's a slam dunk," Howie agrees. • I want to join in as they watch and talk about the game, but it's like they're speaking a foreign language. They might as well be saying: "Ishkabibble coobibabble." • I know nothing about sports. But I know all about animals. • "Hey, Dad," I say, "I know what I want to be when I grow up – a veterinarian." "Yes!" says my dad, "Yes! It's a rimshot! Score!" Sometimes I feel the only way to get my dad's attention is to become a **forward in the New York Knicks.**

Unfortunately, I'm only **4 foot 11 — in Rollerblades.** I most likely would have a hard time passing the Knicks' height requirement.

I Wish I
talk With my
my animal books
this primal need to
do talk!
Whales even
bother to strike
far as 700 miles away!
Biologists don't
find so important to say
maybe
(doubtful!)
they simply have a primal
Which is how I often feel
With my dad
Hey Moby, how about those Knicks?

could figure out how to
dad. You know in one of
I read how all animals have
talk. Even those you don't think talk
up. Conversations as
know what whales could
Biologists guess
eed to ay
Yo, whale here!
Yo, daughter here!
Yo, daughter here!

• Though I feel silly complaining about my dad. I know there are dads who are much (much) worse. I've seen Ricki Lake. I don't think my complaints about my dad would even register on **the Ricki Lake** "gasp-o-meter." I don't know. I don't know **how I feel.** or how I **should** feel. Or **how I feel** about **how I should** feel. I think I feel... like **choco-late.** In particular, I'm **craving** Big Bob's **choco-chunk cookies.** I head into the kitchen—

—**"WAIT"** says my dad. "Put that cookie down!! We're heading out to dinner tonight. Just you and me." "What?" I say. "Your mom has singing rehearsal, and Howie has basketball practice," says my dad "So it's just us tonight. **Where** do you

BIG BOB'S CHOCO-CHUNK

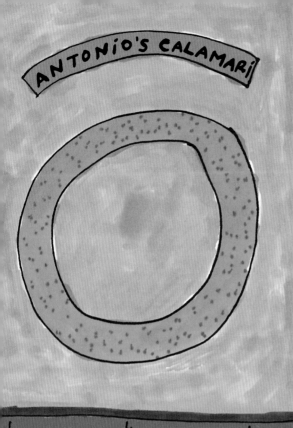

ANTONIO'S CALAMARI

want to go?". "Um, how about **Antonio's**?" I suggest. "They have the best crispy calamari!". Mm-mmm **crispy calamari**," my dad and I say — **at the same time!** · At last, a topic we agree on: crispy calamari. Not much, but it's a start. · "I'll get my coat," I tell my dad, my crispy calamari partner. · "Honey,"

says my dad, "are you sure you can eat calamari?". "What?". "Didn't you tell me you wanted to be a vegetarian?" he says. · "A what?". "A vegetarian," he repeats. · "No, no!" I say. "I said **veterinarian!**". I wonder: will my dad and I ever be able to communicate? **Am I talking in a voice only elves can hear?** · Who knows. Maybe tonight will be different. I know it's only one small meal, yet on some level I'm hoping to create a food bonding experience that will match Little League games everywhere.

We hear you!

Note: Actual size of table in my mind.

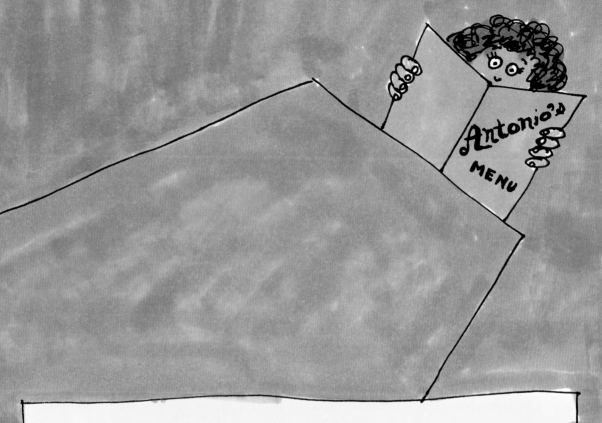

Then finally it happens. **Here I am, with my dad, now, at Antonio's, talking at last.**

Sort of talking.

"New menu," says my dad.

"Looks good," I say.

I am trying to think up things to talk about. Rollerblading? Naaah. Computer games? Uh, don't think so. The difference between amphibians and mammals? Hmm, nope. Uh-oh. What do my dad and I have to say to each other?

I butter my bread.

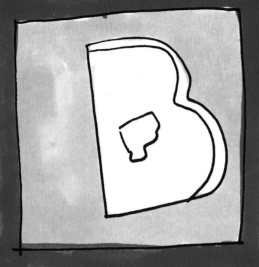

I study my water.

I stare at a lady's weird hairdo.

I look down at my shoes.

• My dad and I have lived in a house 🏠 **together** for 12 ½th years, yet we hardly know each other. I flip through the **photo album** 📷📷📷 **of my mind** for **shared moments.** but they're all of: Mom or Howie, Mom, Mom, Howie, Mom, Howie, Howie, Mom, Howie, Mom. **Then finally** I locate **a Dad memory.** 💡 "Hey, Dad, remember the time I visited you in your office?" I say. "I remember the **swivel chairs** 💺, the **electRONic pencil sharpeners** ✏️, the colored pencils, the **Xerox machine** 🌼🌼🌼. And I remember how at the end of the day you pRomised me if I were good, you'd get me **a gift.** 🎁. 'How about **a pet?**" I asked you. And you said okay. ☺ So, I of course pictured getting a . . .

...**a PUPPY.**

"Yeah, now I remember," says my dad. "And how in the middle of the day you tugged me on the pant leg and asked, 'How am I doing so far, Daddy? Am I doing okay?' **you were so cute**, I just wanted to reach down and **hug you**." • "So, why didn't you, Dad?" • "Didn't I what?" • "Hug me." • "You know, I don't know," he says. • He **tries to smile**, but just like that hug, it never quite comes. • I'm sad/angry/amused/bitter. I want to blurt out everything

I'm feeling, but my **lips feel frozen shut.** I'm as bad as him, I suppose, not being able to say what I feel. But I'm **just** the **daughter.** He's **"The Dad."** He's older and should be better at this, right?

"Do you know what you want?"

I look up. It's the waiter.

"Do you know what you want?" he repeats.

"I'm not sure," I say.

My response echoes **with mega-meaning.**

What do I want? I had big expec- -ations for my dad and dinner tonight—

for us to be like other fathers and daughters Now I wonder how **one small meal** can fill all the hunger inside me.

"Want to start with the fried calamari?" my dad asks.

"Uh, no. Not tonight," I say.

It's not that I don't want the fried calamari. I **fear it.** Ordering an appetizer would mean an extra half hour of conversation that my dad and I would have to fill and thereby remind us that he and I have nothing to say to each other. • In a word: **YIKES!**

"Hey, remember when we went fishing?" my dad asks. • "What? Dad, we never went fishing," I say, annoyed • "I'm kind of joking," says my dad. "I meant at that pet store, later that night, after your office visit. When we got to the pet store, you got to pick out pet fish. You were so happy, remember?" • But what I remember is wondering: FISH? I mean, no way does

a fish = a puppy.
100 fish ≠ 1 puppy
100 fish ≠ ½ puppy.

All I wanted was

1 PUPPY!

I mean, was my dad kidding? • But

...he wasn't. • The ne thing I knew I had 2 new fish roommates: **SPOT** and **SPOT CUBED,** named after their unique markings. SPOT wore this **bizarre spot** across his face. And SPOT CUBED wore three odd spots **on his left —** or would that be his **right ?-** side.

I was bummed I was only getting fish, but I was **psyched** to spend time with my dad.

I was amazed my dad had time to mull over the pros and cons of **blue** (vs) green tiny, shrunken easure chests.

And **pink** (vs) **purple pebbles**. And **square** (vs) **round aquariums**. It made me soooo happy: the sight of a tiny, pretty **plastic mermaid** lying there in the palm of my dad's large hand. Then, when I got home, I had the **strangest reaction.**

• I wanted those fish to **die, die, die.** • An quickly. • I hated those fish because they weren't puppies. You can't take a fish for a walk. Or teach a fish any tricks. Except maybe play dead Fish do that trick well. **EXCEPT MY FISH.** They just would not die. Even after months and months of barely changing their water. • my goal, of course, was for them to choke to death. • I still wanted

a PUPPY. who would love me, lick me, wag happily at the sight of me. I hated those fish for pretending to be pets, for fooling my dad into thinking that the tiny bit of love and attention they offered would be enough. • (**Note:** I wanted more love from a pet. I LOVE LOVE! How come my dad could not see that? Know that? Give me that?) • Soon I had nightmares. I dreamed my **FISH GREW LOCH NESS MONSTER SIZED AND SOUGHT REVENGE ON ME FOR NOT LOVING THEM AS THEY WERE.**

"Yeah," says my dad, smiling at me from across the dinner table. "Yeah, you sure **loved** those fish. I remember, when you went to camp, how much

you missed them. You'd write asking about them."

But what I remember i writing, hoping I'd re

ceive back a fish obit uary.

"I remember," says my dad, "how **unhappy** you were when you found them, you know, passed on."

But what I remember thinking that was the **happiest** day of my your life.

"I know," says my dad, "why don't I buy you some more goldfish after dinner?"

"Well, I ..."

"Oh, wait, I can't. I have to work. But let me give you some money, and you can pick some up tomorrow."

"No thanks."

"Please, take it." ➡   ⬅ "No!"

"Really. My treat." ➡   ⬅ "**NO**!!"

"What?" says my dad, shocked by the extreme **NO-ness** of my response. →

"I have something to admit," I say. "I **hated** those fish. I always wanted them to die. I hated them because they weren't puppies. That's why I never changed their water-I was hoping they'd choke to death. But those fish were, like, bionic. They must have lived for three years!! I was ready to contact Guiness Book of World Records!"

ad sits back and looks t me. "I have something o admit, too," he says. "That summer you went o camp, those fish did ie. And sometimes when ou didn't change the ater, I would. And I'd ind them dead, and each ime I'd replace them ecause I thought you oved them so much." →

"No," I say. "**NOWAY!** I would have noticed! Those fish had **BIZARRE** markings!"

"Well," my dad chuckles, "that's because I made the salesman find fish that looked exactly like Spot and Spot Cubed." • And I picture my dad, a man with a very busy schedule—

— I picture him standing in front of that huge fish tank, filled with hundreds, if not thousands, of fish, and him saying to the salesguy, who has this teeny tiny net,

"I want THAT one! No, no, THAT one!"
• And that's when I knew... • I knew that even if my father STILL never told me if and how fish ever sleep.
... And even if my father STILL never told me how it's possible for ostriches to breathe when their heads are buried in sand... ....I knew... (I guess I knew...)...